**Put Beginning Readers on the Right Track with
ALL ABOARD READING™**

The All Aboard Reading series is especially for beginning readers. Written by noted authors and illustrated in full color, these are books that children really and truly *want* to read—books to excite their imagination, tickle their funny bone, expand their interests, and support their feelings. With four different reading levels, All Aboard Reading lets you choose which books are most appropriate for your children and their growing abilities.

Picture Readers—for Ages 3 to 6
Picture Readers have super-simple texts with many nouns appearing as rebus pictures. At the end of each book are 24 flash cards—on one side is the rebus picture; on the other side is the written-out word.

Level 1—for Preschool through First Grade Children
Level 1 books have very few lines per page, very large type, easy words, lots of repetition, and pictures with visual "cues" to help children figure out the words on the page.

Level 2—for First Grade to Third Grade Children
Level 2 books are printed in slightly smaller type than Level 1 books. The stories are more complex, but there is still lots of repetition in the text and many pictures. The sentences are quite simple and are broken up into short lines to make reading easier.

Level 3—for Second Grade through Third Grade Children
Level 3 books have considerably longer texts, use harder words and more complicated sentences.

All Aboard for happy reading!

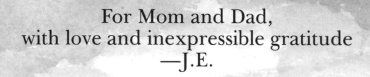

For Mom and Dad,
with love and inexpressible gratitude
—J.E.

For my neighbor Stephanie Wells
—D.D.R.

Text copyright © 1996 by Joan Elste. Illustrations copyright © 1996 by DyAnne DiSalvo-Ryan. All rights reserved. Published by Grosset & Dunlap, Inc., which is a member of The Putnam & Grosset Group, New York. ALL ABOARD READING is a trademark of The Putnam & Grosset Group. GROSSET & DUNLAP is a trademark of Grosset & Dunlap, Inc. Published simultaneously in Canada. Printed in the U.S.A.

Library of Congress Cataloging-in-Publication Data

Elste, Joan.
    True Blue / by Joan Elste ; illustrated by DyAnne DiSalvo-Ryan.
      p.   cm. — (All aboard reading. Level 3)
    Summary: When Blue goes missing, young J. D. goes off to find the dog.
    [1. Dogs—fiction. 2. Hunting—Fiction. 3. Friendship—Fiction.]
  I. DiSalvo-Ryan, DyAnne, ill. II. Title. III. Series.
PZ7.E528Tr 1996   96-1257
[Fic]—dc20   CIP
                                      AC

ISBN 0-448-41264-0 A B C D E F G H I J

ALL
ABOARD
READING™
Level 3
Grades 2-3

True Blue

By Joan Elste
Illustrated by DyAnne DiSalvo-Ryan

Grosset & Dunlap • New York

Chapter 1

My dog has the best sniffing nose east of the Mississippi River. Blue can sniff out a mole in a hole, a 'coon in a hollow, or a 'possum up a tree. He can sniff the breeze and tell which way you are coming from. Then he'll bark to let everybody know you are about to show up.

Blue's best friend is a little dog named Molasses. You can guess how Molasses got his name. He's as slow as the day is long. Molasses belongs to our neighbor, Walter Grange.

Blue always knows when Molasses is coming over. His ears perk up. He sniffs the air and looks down the road. Then suddenly he jumps up, barking. Sure as anything, Walter and Molasses come by in Walter's old pickup truck.

Those two dogs always act like they
have not seen each other in years. They
chase each other around the yard until
Molasses gets tired. That doesn't take
long. Blue tries to get him to play some
more. But old Molasses, he just lies
down, huffing and puffing, his tongue
hanging out a mile.

Molasses still goes hunting with Walter. I can't picture Molasses tracking even a snail. He is nothing like Blue.

Blue is fast. He can pick up a scent right away on account of his great nose. Dad says there's not a better hunting dog in the whole country. Every Saturday during hunting season, off they go together. But one Saturday, Blue went hunting with Dad and didn't come home. That's the day I want to tell you about.

Chapter 2

Mom and I had supper ready. We were beginning to worry. Dad is <u>never</u> late for supper.

At last I heard his footsteps on the porch. I opened the door. I expected Blue to come racing into my arms. But Dad was alone.

"Where's Blue?" I asked. I peered past Dad into the darkness.

"He went after a rabbit or something just as it was getting dark, J.D.," Dad answered. He took off his bright orange vest and cap. "I searched the woods and swamp. I kept calling for him. He didn't come back." Dad sat down at the table with Mom and me. He tried not to look worried, but I could see that he was.

"I heard some shooting. It was out near Walt's place on the other side of the swamp," he said.

"Poachers?" Mom asked. She set the food down on the table.

Now I was worried, too.

"Yesterday Walter said he thought poachers were shooting in the woods," I told them. I'd heard them, too, shooting late at night after Mom and Dad went to sleep.

Maybe you don't know about poachers. But poachers are a big problem here. A dangerous problem. They are people who don't pay attention to hunting laws. They'll hunt on anybody's land, day or night, even if you have No Trespassing signs up. And they'll shoot at anything that moves. Anything!

"Do you think Blue went after poachers?" I asked Dad. I was scared. "Blue's never run off before. Maybe he's hurt. Maybe he's stuck somewhere and can't get home." I set my fork down on the table. I couldn't eat anymore.

"I don't think Blue would leave our property," he said. "It's too dark to look tonight, J.D. Blue is a smart pup. He won't go far and will probably wander on home later. If not, I'll look for him again tomorrow. Don't worry."

But I did worry. That night, I lay awake in my bed. Blue's spot near the bottom of the bed was cold. No lump warmed my feet. Nothing stirred when I rolled over and cried into my pillow.

Chapter 3

The next morning Blue still had not come home. Fog and light rain drifted through the trees. Before Mom and Dad were even up, I got dressed. I decided I was going to find Blue.

I walked to the edge of the woods and searched out all of Blue's favorite places. I called his name again and again. The sound of my voice seemed to travel only a few feet. Then it hit the wall of fog. I wanted to look further, but I knew Mom and Dad wouldn't like me going into the woods with poachers around. Finally I walked home, sad and discouraged.

Later that morning, Walter stopped by.

"I heard shooting again last night," he told Dad. "I'm worried. I'm sure poachers have been up on the hill."

"I heard them too," Dad said.

Walter went on. "This is getting pretty serious. Those stupid fools were on my land last year. They built a fire and nearly burned my woods down."

Walter scratched the beard stubble on his chin. "By the way, you haven't seen Molasses, have you? He wandered off yesterday evening and never came home. He's old. Likes to be by himself sometimes. But it's not like Molasses to stay out all night."

"Blue never came home either!" I said. "He's never done that."

"I was going to look for him later on," Dad said. "I wish this fog would lift off some."

I didn't tell him I'd already been out looking for Blue.

"Well, keep an eye out for Molasses when you go. I'm going to check out my side of the swamp," Walter told us. "And don't you worry, J.D." Walter started the motor. "Them dogs are smart. They'll stay out of trouble."

After Walter left I tried to keep busy. I watched Dad clean his rifle. I tried to work on a story I was writing for school. Nothing worked. I knew something was wrong.

By late afternoon, I couldn't stand it any longer. Poachers or not, I had to go look for Blue.

Chapter 4

The woods were very still. It was almost like they were waiting for something to happen. Even the birds were quiet. Now and then I heard a dead branch fall.

As I got near the other side of the swamp, I thought I heard a sound. But I never got to find out what it was. Right then I tripped on a rotten log. Down I fell, into the mud.

After that, I walked carefully. The fog seemed to be thinning. It was hugging the ground more. I crossed over into Walter's woods. The No Trespassing signs had been torn off the trees. They were lying on the ground. There was a small ring of ashes by the stream. Poachers had been camping here!

I sat on a log to rest. Without warning, the hair on the back of my neck prickled. I got this funny feeling, sort of like Blue was thinking of me. So I started whistling for him.

Then I heard a loud crashing
through the woods. Suddenly, there he
was! Blue came bursting through the
bushes barking.

"Blue!" I cried. I threw my arms around him. We rolled on the ground, just loving each other to pieces. "I was so scared!" I scolded him.

Then I saw that the side of his coat was really dark and sticky. There was dried blood in his fur!

I looked for a cut. I couldn't find one. Blue was acting so happy. Maybe he'd just been rolling in something dead, which dogs like to do.

I turned to walk home, slapping my leg for Blue to follow. Instead, he just sat down.

"Come on, Blue," I called. "Let's go home." Blue didn't move. He put his front paws out and lay down. I went back to grab him by his collar. He pulled away and ran off into the woods.

"Blue!" I yelled.

What was going on here?

Chapter 5

I whistled a few times. Blue came back. He stood away from me and barked. I couldn't get him to follow, no matter how I tried. He just ran off again.

If only I had a rope with me. But I never had to put a leash on Blue before. He always obeyed. So I decided to see what he was up to. It was starting to get dark. But at least the fog was lifting.

Blue was fast. And it was hard for me to follow him. But it seemed whenever I lost track of him, he always came back to get me.

A big white hunter's moon slid high along the treetops. The fog was nearly gone by now. But it was getting chilly. I buttoned up my jacket.

Blue ran deeper and deeper into the woods. I was growing tired of his game. I was hungry, too. And I bet Mom and Dad were worrying about me. "Shoot!" I said aloud. "Why didn't I leave a note?"

I was really mad now. "Come back here, you stupid dog!" I yelled. "Or I'm going to let you stay here all night!"

I couldn't hear or see him. I whistled again. But this time, Blue didn't come back.

Chapter 6

I was getting madder. Maybe I could grab Blue by the collar and use my belt as a leash. Just wait till I found that dog!

It didn't take long. I walked through some thick underbrush and there I saw him.

Blue was lying next to what looked like a small pile of dirt. "No more games now, Blue," I said, inching up on him. But then I stopped. Blue was whining.

The pile of dirt suddenly heaved slightly. At first I thought my eyes were playing tricks. Then I saw. The pile of dirt was a dog!

"Molasses!" I cried. I dropped to my knees. I bent over the still body. Molasses was near dead from bleeding. A bullet was in his back leg. His coat was full of blood. The poachers had shot him! Blue must have been lying next to him all night and day to keep him warm.

I took off my coat and put it around Molasses. He was so weak. He whimpered as I lifted him into my arms.

Molasses is a small dog. Even so, he was heavy. I could barely carry him. I walked carefully, trying not to fall or cry. But I didn't know if I could get Molasses home in time. His breathing was so slow. He seemed to grow heavier with each step I took.

Blue did not leave my side now. He walked close by, watching my every move.

"I can't carry him anymore!" I
sobbed and sat on the ground. The limp
body of Molasses lay in my lap. I cried
for what seemed like a long time. There
wasn't any time to run home and get
Dad. By then, old Molasses would be
dead. So I just sobbed and sobbed and
rocked poor Molasses in my arms.

Chapter 7

I wished with all my heart for a miracle. And then, for no reason at all, Blue sat bolt upright. The hair on his back stood up and he growled.

I was scared. What if poachers were coming? What if they shot me, thinking I was a deer or something? I bet they shot Molasses thinking he was a 'coon. I sat very still and held my breath.

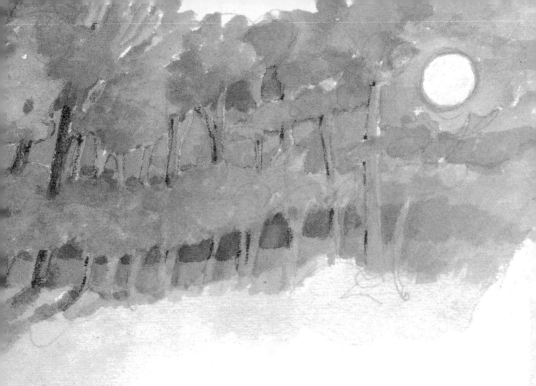

Blue tore past me into the woods. Then I heard the sound of my name floating on the night air like music.

"J.D.!" Dad cried when he reached us. Blue was leaping and jumping all over him. "Your Mom and I were worried sick."

Then he saw Molasses and gathered
him gently in his arms. "Oh my
goodness!" he said. "Looks like you both
need some tending to."

In ten minutes we were home. We lay Molasses on the floor in front of the woodstove. Dad called the vet, but he was away on a fishing trip. So Mom warmed a pot of water to clean the wound, while Dad called Walter.

Walter came and they both worked hard over poor Molasses. At last they got the bullet out.

"He's one tough old hound dog," Walter said to Dad. "A bullet in the leg isn't going to keep him down." I could see tears in his eyes. "Lucky J.D. found him."

"Blue found him," I said sleepily. "He knew Molasses was in trouble. So he went looking for him."

"But he was clear across the swamp and deep in the woods on the far end of my land," Walter said. "Blue's never been over there."

"Blue can sniff out anything. You've seen him."

"It still amazes me," Walter answered. He scratched the top of his head.

"And he kept Molasses warm all night," I told them both. "He was lying almost on top of him. I saw it."

We could see Walter was still pretty upset. Dad threw his arm around Walter. "Why, I'd do as much for you, Walt," he teased.

Walter laughed. Then he wiped his eyes with his sleeve. "I've had that old hound longer than I care to remember," he said. "I don't know what I'd do without him."

"He'll be fine," Dad told him. "The vet will be home tomorrow. Take Molasses over just to check. I think we did a good job. Lucky we got him here when we did."

"Thanks, J.D.," Walter said. He
picked up Molasses and tenderly
wrapped him in a blanket. "And thank
you too, Blue."

Blue slapped his tail a few tired
times. He knew Walter was praising
him.

By the time Walter left, Blue was sound asleep at the foot of my bed. I watched him whimpering and kicking in his sleep. I pulled back the covers and slid into bed. I was sure Blue was chasing a mole to its hole, a 'coon to its hollow, or a 'possum up a tree.